Ballerina
Holly and the Silver

Welcome to the world of Enchantia!

I have always loved to dance. The captivating
music and wonderful stories of ballet are so
inspiring. So come with me and let's follow
Holly on her magical adventures in
Enchantia, where the stories of dance will
take you on a very special journey.

p.s. Turn to the back to learn a special
dance step from me...

Special thanks to
Linda Chapman and
Katie May

First published in Great Britain by HarperCollins Children's Books 2009
HarperCollins Children's Books is a division of HarperCollins Publishers Ltd,
77-85 Fulham Palace Road, Hammersmith, London W6 8JB

The HarperCollins website address is
www.harpercollins.co.uk

1

Text copyright © HarperCollins Children's Books 2009
Illustrations by Katie May
Illustrations copyright © HarperCollins Children's Books 2009

MAGIC BALLERINA™ and the 'Magic Ballerina' logo are
trademarks of HarperCollins Publishers Ltd.

ISBN-13 978 0 00 732320 3

Printed and bound in England by
Clays Ltd, St Ives plc

Mixed Sources
Product group from well-managed
forests and other controlled sources
www.fsc.org Cert no. SW-COC-1806
© 1996 Forest Stewardship Council

FSC is a non-profit international organisation established to promote the
responsible management of the world's forests. Products carrying the FSC
label are independently certified to assure consumers that they come
from forests that are managed to meet the social, economic and
ecological needs of present and future generations.

Find out more about HarperCollins and the environment at
www.harpercollins.co.uk/green

Magic Ballerina™

Holly and the Silver Unicorn

Darcey Bussell

HarperCollins *Children's Books*

ENCH
Royal Palace
Sugar Plum Fairy's Cottage
The Village
The Land of SWEETS
THEATRE
Theatre

To Phoebe and Zoe, as they are the inspiration behind Magic Ballerina.

Contents

Prologue   9

Dancing on Stage   11

The Enchanted Carousel   26

In the High Mountains   36

Dancing Magic   46

Captured!   60

Breaking the Spell   71

Saying Sorry   83

Darcey's Magical Masterclass   92

Prologue

*In the soft, pale light, the girl stood
with her head bent and her hands
held lightly in front of her.
There was a moment's silence and then
the first notes of the music began.
For as long as the girl could remember
music had seemed to tell her of
another world – a magical, exciting
world – that lay far, far away.
She always felt if she could just
close her eyes and lose herself,
then she would get there.
Maybe this time. As the music
swirled inside her, she swept
her arms above her head, rose on to
her toes and began to dance…*

Dancing on Stage

Holly Wilde stood with her class, waiting to go on stage, as beautiful music filled the theatre. Her teacher, Madame Za-Za, had choreographed a forest ballet for their Christmas production and this dress rehearsal was the first time the girls had danced properly in their costumes.

"Oh, I hope we don't get anything

wrong," whispered Chloe, Holly's friend.

The other girls nodded anxiously.

"I'm so nervous!" said Alice.

"Me too," agreed Lily.

Holly tucked a loose
strand of brown hair
back into her bun and
moved a few steps
away. She didn't feel
nervous. After all, they
were only dancing the
part of the *corps de ballet*.

The *corps* were supposed to dance
together with no one standing out or being
different. A small sigh escaped Holly. She
would have loved to have got a main part,
but she had only been at Madame Za-Za's

for six months and all the bigger roles had gone to the older girls.

She looked around at her classmates – like her, they were all wearing long white dresses to dance the parts of sylphs – fairy-like creatures with wings who led people astray. But, unlike her, the other girls were whispering nervously together. It made her feel very different.

But things are different for you, Holly reminded herself.

Her mum and dad were both professional ballet dancers and whilst that was exciting, it didn't make for the easiest of lives. Holly had spent most of her early years travelling around with either one or the other of them. Six months ago, they had decided

that she needed to put down roots in one
place, so she'd been living with her aunt
and uncle ever since. She was getting used
to it and now, at least, she'd made a friend
in Chloe. Her first proper friend. *Well, in
this world*, she thought.

An image of a dancing white cat flashed
into Holly's mind and she smiled. For she
had a secret – a pair of magic red ballet
shoes that whisked her away to the land of
Enchantia, where the characters from all the
different ballets lived. Holly couldn't wait
to go back, but so far the shoes hadn't
sparkled with magic since her first visit.

Still, there was plenty of time for that, she
told herself and snapping out of her reverie,
she practised a *plié*, finishing by rising up

on her toes, her free arm moving out gracefully to the side.

Chloe came over. "How are you feeling?"

Holly looked at her in surprise. "Fine."

"Really?" Chloe whispered. "You're not nervous?"

"There's nothing to be nervous about, is there?" Holly said, as she heard a change in the music. "Come on, it's almost time to go on. We'd better join the others!"

They hurried over to get ready.

When they danced on to the stage, the lights were so bright, Holly couldn't see anything in the darkness of the auditorium, but she knew Madame Za-Za would be out there, watching them. Holly did just as the others were doing, moving forward with tiny running steps, sweeping her arms down, and then up and turning round, before continuing onwards again.

But gradually the music took hold and the urge to dance as well as she possibly could started to build inside her. She tried to ignore it at first, but it grew fiercer and stronger. When the others stood on their toes, their arms in the air, Holly held her position for a moment longer, and as they moved into a circle and stood on one leg,

she lifted hers higher than anyone else's.
She wanted to be different. She didn't want
to be just the same. She wanted to dance
her very best!

At the end of the dance, the girls all ran offstage in their line. Holly stopped in the wings and took a deep, happy breath. She felt wonderful!

She vaguely noticed a few of the other dancers giving her cross looks as they headed off to the changing rooms, but she didn't really take them in until Chloe came over to her. "Holly! How could you?" she said.

"What?" said Holly in surprise.

"Dance like that. You were showing off like crazy!"

"No, I wasn't," Holly protested.

"But you were!" Chloe went on. "You know we're supposed to be dancing together, all doing the same thing. But you were dancing differently. Madame Za-Za's going to be really mad."

Holly felt a flash of anger as the buzzing happiness she had been feeling after the dance was abruptly extinguished. "I was only dancing as well as I could," she said, aware that a certain amount of haughtiness had crept into her voice. "What's wrong with that?"

"It's not what you do when you're dancing in the *corps*," Chloe said. "You know it's not." Her voice softened. "We're meant to act like a team."

Holly felt angry and she marched away, grabbing her old red ballet shoes from where she had left them at the side of the stage. How could Chloe tell her off like that? They were supposed to be friends. How dare she say she was showing off!

But you were, weren't you? a little voice in her head pointed out.

I was just dancing the best I could, Holly thought defensively. *We're supposed to do that.*

No, she realised, her temper finally calming. *In the corps we are supposed to dance together.*

As the anger drained out of her, she started to feel bad. What was Madame Za-Za going to say? And it wasn't just that. She'd snapped at Chloe. And the other girls, how must they be feeling?

Holly swallowed hard and stopped. She had reached the large scenery hall and the backstage entrance to the theatre. The stage-door keeper sat in a little cubicle letting the dancers and stage crew in and out.

"Are you OK, sweetheart?" he asked.
"You look rather flushed."

"I'm just hot," lied Holly.

"You should be glad of the warmth. It's
snowing outside," he commented.

"Snowing!" gasped Holly, her own problems
momentarily forgotten. "Can I go and see?"

The stage-door keeper frowned. "You're
not really allowed outside the theatre when
you're here with the school."

"But it's the interval in a minute. I'm not
needed on stage. I'll only be a few seconds.
Oh, I could really do with some fresh air.
Please? I won't do anything stupid," Holly
begged.

"Oh, all right," he gave in. "But don't go
too far and if you're not back inside in one

minute, I'm coming to get you. Deal?"

"Deal!" said Holly, quickly hurrying outside.

The stage door opened into a quiet back street. The sky was dark and the only light came from a nearby golden street lamp. Snow was falling in big silent flakes, settling on the ground like a white carpet.

"Oh, wow!" Holly breathed, putting her hand out and feeling the flakes land icily on her fingers.

She watched them swirl down and suddenly was filled with the urge to dance in the snow. She couldn't in her performance shoes – she would be in even more trouble if she got those wet and dirty. Pulling off her white shoes, she put on her old red ones, tied up the ribbons and jumped to her feet. She could hear the music faintly from inside the theatre as the first act finished and she began to twirl and dance.

Suddenly she became aware that it wasn't just her hands and arms that were tingling where the snowflakes were landing, it was her feet too.

She glanced down and saw the shoes were shining as if they were covered with bright jewels.

"Enchantia!" she gasped. "I'm going to Enchantia again!"

The Enchanted Carousel

A bright twinkling cloud of blue, silver, lilac, pink and gold sparkles swept around Holly and she was spun up into the air. A few seconds later, she was put gently back down. Even before the sparkles had cleared she could feel the difference. The air was warm and there was grass beneath her feet.

The cloud around her vanished. She was

standing in the garden of the Royal Palace. She'd been here before. Suddenly the White Cat came hurrying out. He was standing on his hind legs and was wearing a golden waistcoat and black boots.

"White Cat!" Holly cried in delight.

He turned round. "Holly! Oh, my ears and whiskers!" He jumped high in the air, crossing his feet over five times before landing and running over. On the way, he leaped into a *grand jeté* and landed in front of her. Grabbing her by the hands, he swung her round.

She laughed. It was wonderful to be back in Enchantia.

"I'm so glad to see you!" the cat cried. "Oh, my shimmering whiskers, Holly! This is the best surprise ever. You're bound to be able to help!"

"Why? What's going on?" asked Holly.

"It's the Wicked Fairy again," the White Cat said, his usually cheerful face looking suddenly worried.

Holly shuddered as she pictured the Wicked Fairy with her hooked warty nose, black wand and long cloak. She'd met her in her first adventure in Enchantia, when she'd tried to spoil Princess Aurelia's wedding anniversary. She was one of the few really horrible characters in Enchantia.

"What's she been doing?" Holly asked.

"I'll show you!" The White Cat waved his long fluffy tail once and then used the end to draw a circle on the ground. Sparks

shot up into the air and a mist formed
inside the circle he'd drawn.

As the mist cleared, Holly saw a carousel –
a black iron merry-go-round with a spiky
top. It was in the grounds of a dark

creepy-looking castle and had some amazing creatures on it – a giant swan and a dove, a magnificent stag, a brown bear and a sea dragon. There was one empty space left.

Holly looked at the White Cat.

"That's the Wicked Fairy's Castle, isn't it?"

"Yes. And it's her carousel. She has been collecting all the most amazing creatures in the land and putting them on it."

"So they're real animals?" said Holly, looking at the lifeless carousel creatures with their blank, staring eyes.

The White Cat wrung his front paws together. "Yes. They were all free to move about until she enchanted them. At the moment the magic is only temporary, so they could come back to life, but when the Wicked Fairy fills the final space, the magic will become permanent and then all those wonderful creatures will be lost forever."

"But, that's dreadful!" exclaimed Holly.

"I know!" the White Cat said. "The

trouble is no one knows quite how to break the spell. The King's magicians are working on it right now, but while they do, we need to stop her from catching the last creature – the Silver Unicorn."

"A unicorn!" breathed Holly, her mind filled with a picture of a beautiful white horse with a long glittering horn.

The White Cat nodded. "King Tristan sent him an invitation to come to the court so he could be protected, but the Silver Unicorn is proud and stubborn and he refused. King Tristan wants to try to find him, but it's tricky. The unicorn has magic that allows him to become invisible, to hide from people trying to spy on him. The only way of finding him is to track him down, but the High Mountains, where he lives, are dangerous and the unicorn can gallop incredibly swiftly."

"Maybe the Wicked Fairy won't be able to find him then, either?" said Holly hopefully.

"We were hoping that, but she has sent a large number of hunters out." The White

Cat drew another circle with his tail. This
time, Holly saw a range of jagged mountains
with snow-topped peaks and misty slopes
covered with pine trees. The picture got
closer and closer as if it was a film zooming
in, until Holly could see hunters with hard,
cruel faces stealthily creeping through the
trees, sharp swords by their sides, nets and

ropes attached to their backpacks. She caught her breath. The thought of them catching the unicorn was awful.

"We have to find him before they do!" she declared.

The White Cat nodded. "Legend suggests that young girls have a certain power over unicorns, so maybe you'll be able to persuade him to come here until the magicians have worked out how to break the carousel's enchantment and free the other creatures."

"Let's go to the mountains straight away, then," said Holly, determination rising up inside her. They couldn't let the Wicked Fairy's hunters catch the Silver Unicorn – she and the White Cat had to find him first!

In the High Mountains

The White Cat twitched his long whiskers. Silver sparks flew off them and surrounded Holly and the cat. They spun away.

The magic set them down in the middle of a forest. The air was chillier than it had been in the palace gardens and seemed thinner when Holly breathed it in. Pine needles crackled beneath her feet. Glancing upwards, she saw the tall slim tree trunks. They seemed to stretch right up into the sky. Holly's skin prickled with goosebumps. It felt like a very magical place.

"We must watch out for the sylphs who live here," the White Cat warned. "They don't usually get involved with the rest of us in Enchantia. The only people who see them are those who come out into these woods. The sylphs lead them astray into bogs and dark places." He shivered. "They're beautiful but strange creatures. Hopefully we won't come across any of them. Anyway, let's get moving and try and find the Silver Unicorn."

Holly nodded and they set off into the trees.

The misty forest seemed to go on forever.
They followed one path and then another,
climbing over tangles of brambles and
fallen tree trunks and tripping over roots.
Soon they were both scratched and bruised.
But Holly didn't think about stopping.
They *had* to find the unicorn!

"Look!" the White Cat hissed, pointing.

Holly followed his gaze. Just ahead of them a silver shape was moving through the trees.

"It's the unicorn!" she breathed. "We've found him!"

"Hurrah!" said the White Cat, spinning round. "Will you go and talk to him, Holly? He might gallop off without listening if he sees me. He won't hurt you, I promise. Unicorns are very gentle, even if they are stubborn and proud."

Holly went forward. "Hello," she called softly. "Silver Unicorn?"

The unicorn looked round. He was beautiful. His eyes were like deep forest pools and his mane and tail swept to the floor and were threaded through with shining hairs of pure silver.

"Who are you?" he asked.

"Holly, I'm from the human world. I own the red ballet shoes."

The unicorn nodded. "I have heard about

them." He looked at her curiously. "What do you want with me?"

"I want you to come to the Royal Palace," Holly told him, "to stop the Wicked Fairy from catching you."

The unicorn snorted proudly. "I am the Silver Unicorn. I do not need the King's protection!"

"But the Wicked Fairy has hunters out looking for you, as we speak," Holly said desperately. "If they catch you, the enchantment on the carousel will never be broken. Please, come!"

"No!" The unicorn tossed his mane. "They will never catch me!" In a flash he was gone, galloping away through the trees.

Holly stared after him in dismay. The White Cat came hurrying up to her.

"He just wouldn't listen," said Holly. "The legend can't be right."

"Maybe you actually need to touch him for the magic to work?" fretted the White Cat. "I should have suggested that." He twisted the end of his tail round anxiously. "What are we going to do now? I suppose we'd better go back."

"No!" said Holly quickly. "If you think it might work, I'll try again. Let's go after him. We can't give up yet!"

They hurried on through the trees, but there was no further sign of the unicorn. As they fought their way down a tangled path, they heard some music coming from the left. Holly looked round. "What's that?"

"I don't know," the White Cat replied.

Holly pushed her way through the trees. Something white was moving around in a glade ahead of them. For a moment, Holly wondered if it was the unicorn again. She broke into a run, but as she reached the edge of the trees, she stopped.

A group of about twenty beautiful girls were dancing in two circles on the short grass. They were all wearing white dresses, very like the one Holly had on and they had gauzy wings too, only theirs were real! Their hair was tied back in buns and they had white ballet shoes on their

feet. They moved as if they were floating, their feet hardly seeming to touch the ground.

"Sylphs!" Holly breathed.

Dancing Magic

"Oh, no!" Holly heard the White Cat mutter, but she ignored him. The sylphs were weaving between each other. Their wings and dresses shimmered. Holly didn't think she had ever seen a more mesmerising sight.

"Holly, come on!" The White Cat pulled at her arm. "Sylphs like to be left alone."

Holly shook her head. Something was going wrong with the dance. She could see it! The sylphs were weaving in and out, but when they stopped and faced each other there was always one sylph left out. The music started to jangle and sound discordant. The sylphs exclaimed in frustration and the music stopped altogether. "It's not working!" said one.

"What are you doing?" Holly asked, walking into the glade.

The sylphs turned and stared at her in astonishment. "Who are you?"

"Oh, Holly!" said the White Cat, bounding after her and standing at her side. He looked round at the sylphs.

"Greetings!" he said, sweeping into an elegant bow. The sylphs rose on their toes, then moved backwards with tiny steps into a tighter group, their eyes wary.

Holly saw that a sylph was lying in the centre of the glade. She looked in pain.

"Are you all right?" Holly
asked quickly.

The other sylphs
fluttered their wings
unhappily.

"My wing's been
damaged," the injured sylph replied,
showing her ripped left wing.

"One of the hunters who was in the
woods fired an arrow at Melina," said
another, stepping forward. "We can do a
healing dance, but it needs twenty of us
and the magic is not working with only
nineteen. We'll try again. If you would
leave us, please." She and the other sylphs
looked pointedly at Holly and the White
Cat.

"Of course," the cat said, backing away.

But Holly didn't move. "But maybe I could help? I mean, I can't dance on my pointes and I'm not as good as you, but if it would help to have someone else…"

Her voice trailed off. The sylphs were staring at her as if she had said something astonishing.

"I'm sorry," she said, going red. "I didn't mean to offend you. It was probably a stupid idea. I… I just thought…"

The sylph who had spoken before, stepped towards her. "*You* would help *us*?"

"Of course," said Holly. "Why wouldn't I?"

The sylph frowned. "Most people in Enchantia avoid us. They do not like us. They would certainly never stop to help."

"Well, I'm not like that," said Holly. "I'll help."

The sylphs gathered and whispered to each other, then the first sylph turned.

"Thank you. We would be very grateful for your help." Around her, all the other sylphs were smiling now too and the tension in the air had disappeared.

"My name is Ava," said the first sylph.

"I'm Holly," said Holly. "And this is the White Cat. What do you want me to do?"

"We'll show you."

Ava and the other sylphs performed the dance. Holly watched carefully. She really wanted to get it right and help heal Melina's injured wing.

"Are you ready?" Ava asked when they had been over the steps with her several times.

Holly nodded and walked into the circle. As they took the first few steps, faint music magically floated through the clearing. Holly followed Ava, keeping her movements as light as possible, her arms graceful. Remembering how she had made a mess of things back in the real world when she had been dancing in the *corps*, she tried to dance exactly as the sylphs were dancing, matching her movements to theirs.

The dancers changed direction and then faced their partners. The music grew louder and the dancing, faster. Holly spun round.

Suddenly a shout went up. Holly stared
as Melina flew into the air. Her wing had
healed! She posed in an *arabesque* on one
leg, just as if she was
standing on
the solid
ground, her
wings
fluttering
and keeping
her up.

"Wow!" Holly
gasped.

The other sylphs
laughed in delight as Melina flew down.

"You're better!"

"Your wing has healed!"

Melina gently embraced Holly. "Thank you so much."

Holly beamed.

"So why are you in these woods?" Ava asked her. "We don't get many visitors to these parts." Her face darkened. "Apart from hunters."

Holly glanced at the White Cat, wondering if it was OK to explain. He nodded.

"Well, it's because of the hunters that we're here," said Holly. "We're trying to find the Silver Unicorn before they do." And she told the sylphs all about the Wicked Fairy's enchanted carousel. "We found the unicorn, but he wouldn't listen to me," she finished. "He galloped off, so now we're trying to find him again."

Ava looked thoughtful. "We don't usually involve ourselves in the affairs of Enchantia, but it would be our pleasure to foil the hunters in their attempts. We will help you find the unicorn." She turned to the others. "Go, my friends. Discover where the Silver Unicorn is and bring the news back."

Within seconds, the clearing had emptied as the other sylphs flew away.

"Are you sure they'll be able to find him? He gallops so fast," said Holly.

Ava smiled. "And we fly fast too. If he is in the woods, we will find him for you. I promise."

°ⓞ⠂*. ☆ ⠂ⓞ⠂*. ☆ ⠂ⓞ⠂*.☆ ⠐ⓞ⠂*. °

Within ten minutes, the sylphs returned with the news that they had found the Silver Unicorn about a mile away.

"How will we get there?" asked Holly.

"Dance and follow us, and you will end up travelling a mile in only a few minutes. Our magic will help you," replied Ava.

"Thank you," the White Cat said gratefully.

Ava turned and clapped her hands. "Sylphs, away!"

Music flooded through the trees. "Follow us!" Ava called to the White Cat and Holly.

Holly could see a sylph through the trees. She danced towards her, holding the cat's hand. The sylph seemed to slip away, but then there was another and another, hovering and vanishing. Holly felt a warmth wrap around her and she didn't get out of breath at all as she and the cat followed the white figures. It was the easiest dancing she had ever done.

Suddenly the music stopped. Holly looked around and realised they were in a completely different part of the woods, with smaller trees and larger bramble bushes. The sylphs had vanished. She saw a silver shape through the trees, so she ran forward.

"It's the unicorn!" she cried. "Come on, Cat!"

Captured!

As Holly entered the clearing where the Silver Unicorn was grazing, she saw a movement in the trees on the far side of the clearing, and wondered if it was one of the sylphs. But she didn't have time to think about that now.

The unicorn lifted his head. "Oh, it's you

again," he said grumpily. "You might as well stop wasting your time following me. I told you, I'm not coming with you to the palace."

"Please, just listen to me." Holly held out her hand. If she could only touch him…

But the unicorn backed away, shaking his head, as if he could read her mind. "I don't need protecting. I'm not coming!"

"Wait!" cried Holly as he plunged towards the trees. Then suddenly several things happened at once. A group of men burst into the clearing and a giant net was thrown over the unicorn! He reared and fought, his horn and hooves getting caught within the netting, as Holly screamed. The White Cat bounded out and landed protectively beside her as she started running forward, shouting, "Stop it!" whilst the men struggled to get the unicorn under control.

One of the hunters suddenly lifted a crystal orb and a cloud of green smoke suddenly surrounded him, the other men and the unicorn. And then they were whisked away. Where they had been standing was now just an empty clearing! Holly was aghast.

"Oh, my shimmering whiskers!" cried the White Cat, jumping in agitation. "They've captured him! Whatever are we going to do now?"

Holly's heart was beating fast. "They'll take him to the Wicked Fairy's Castle. We've got to go after him!"

"But it will be dangerous!"

The cat's tail swished from side to side in agitation as a silvery voice rang out. "We'll come with you!"

Holly turned to see the sylphs standing behind them. They looked angry.

"We were watching from the trees," Ava explained, hands on her hips. "No magical creature should ever be treated in such a way. Those hunters need teaching a lesson. We'll help you free him."

"Thank you!" cried Holly. She had no idea how they could possibly free the unicorn, but it made her feel much better to know the sylphs were coming too.

"Hold hands and I'll use my magic to take us there," said the White Cat. He whisked around the clearing, drawing a big circle with his tail. Silver sparks

started to rise up from the grass. Everyone
jumped inside the circle, held hands and
the next minute, they were whisked
away!

Holly, the White Cat and all of the sylphs
came to rest in the cover of a small copse of
trees in the gardens of the Wicked Fairy's
Castle. Black and green flags flew from the
turrets and on the grass stood the dreadful
iron carousel. In front of it, the hunters
were trying to control the unicorn. He'd
fought free of the net, but they had got a
rope round his neck and had attached it to
a metal ring in the ground. It was holding
him fast!

Holly's stomach somersaulted as the Wicked Fairy came marching out of the castle, cackling. "You caught him!" she cried, rubbing her hands. "The last of the magical creatures for my carousel. Very good. Very good indeed!"

The unicorn reared up and she laughed. "You can fight all you like, Unicorn, but there is no escape from me. I will now fetch my spell book, then you will be added to the carousel. Once you are in position, the enchantment will be sealed forever!" She swung round and went back inside.

"What are we going to do?" hissed the White Cat.

Holly didn't know. "We can't get near enough to untie him. If only there was a way to distract the hunters..."

She broke off. "Ava! Could you and the others use your magic dancing to distract them, perhaps? Then the White Cat and I might be able to get close enough to untie the unicorn."

Ava nodded. "Yes, we can do that."

She called to the other sylphs, who were hovering and floating in the trees and explained the plan. They formed a line and rose on to their pointes straight away.

"We're ready," said Melina.

"Then let's go!" cried Holly.

As the sylphs danced out of the trees, the hunters pointed and stared. A few of them reached for their swords, but before they could draw them, the magic worked and their hands fell to their sides. They seemed to forget all about what they were supposed to be doing. The sylphs weaved in and out of them, moving gradually away from the carousel – and the unicorn.

Holly and the White Cat raced across the grass.

"It's you!" the Silver Unicorn said in amazement, as Holly threw herself down and started trying to untie the rope, while the White Cat kept watch for the Wicked Fairy.

"Yes, we've come to rescue you!" she said, her fingers tugging frantically at the knot.

The unicorn whinnied. "I should have listened to you! I should have gone to the Royal Palace!"

"We can still get you there," said Holly. She had almost untied the rope. But just then there was a wild shriek.

"Holly!" the White Cat cried in alarm.

Holly looked up and gasped. The Wicked Fairy was running out of the castle and heading straight towards them!

Breaking the Spell

"What are you doing? I order you to get back to your positions!" the Wicked Fairy yelled at the hunters.

But the sylphs' magic held them fast. They gazed wonderingly at Ava and the others, seeming to see and hear nothing else.

Desperately, Holly tugged at the rope as

the Wicked Fairy focused on her and lifted her wand. "Stop that!" the fairy screeched.

The White Cat leaped in front of Holly, turning and spinning as fast as he could. The Wicked Fairy fired a jet of green flames at him. He leaped into the air, jumping high above it.

"I'll get you, cat!" the Wicked Fairy snarled, shooting another blast of green fire.

The White Cat sprang upwards again, tucking his knees high. He landed and immediately twirled away. At the same moment, the rope slipped out from the ring. "You're free!" Holly cried to the unicorn.

The unicorn charged forward – straight at the Wicked Fairy! As he reached her, his long horn caught in her cloak and dress. With a squawk, she was swung up into the air and the unicorn whinnied triumphantly. He galloped forward while she screamed, "Let me go! Put me down!"

The unicorn did as she asked. He stopped abruptly in front of the carousel and dumped her right into the empty space.

Instantly, the iron carousel split in half

with a loud CRACK!

"Oh, my glittering tail! Putting *her* into the empty space has broken the enchantment!" cried the White Cat.

Holly clasped her hands and watched in astonishment as all the creatures suddenly came back to life. The swan hissed, the bear growled, the sea dragon roared and the dove flapped her wings. Then they all turned to the Wicked Fairy! She

stumbled to her feet, half falling off the
carousel, not having the chance to raise her
wand. The creatures leaped towards her. She
ran back to the castle with the swan
and the dove pecking at
her from the air and
the sea dragon,
bear and stag
charging
behind her.
The Wicked
Fairy slammed
the door shut in
their faces.
"We did it!" cried the
White Cat, leaping into the air
with joy. "The enchantment's broken!"

The unicorn appeared beside them. "It won't take the Wicked Fairy long to get herself together and come out again." He knelt down on to his front legs. "Get on my back and I'll take you away."

"But what about the others?" demanded Holly.

"They'll be fine," said the unicorn and even as he spoke, the dove and swan were flapping away and the bear, stag and dragon were racing into the woods. "Come on! We must go!"

Holly grabbed the unicorn's mane and threw herself on to his silvery back. The White Cat leaped up lightly behind her. Within a few bounds, the unicorn was into the trees and away.

The world seemed to fly by around them as they raced through the forest, until finally they slowed down to stop, deep in the woods.

"I will leave you here," he said. "We are far from the Wicked Fairy's castle and you will be safe. I must go on to the High Mountains and I presume you will be going back to the Royal Palace."

Holly nodded and slipped off his back. "It's been lovely meeting you."

"Thank you for rescuing me," the unicorn said. "And I'm sorry to have put you both in so much danger." His dark eyes looked troubled. "I should have listened to you. My pride almost cost you and me – and all the other magic creatures – our lives. I'm sorry."

"Everyone makes mistakes," Holly said softly. For a moment, a picture of her behaviour at the theatre back at home flashed into her mind: dancing on the stage, snapping at Chloe...

She touched the unicorn's soft neck.

The unicorn nuzzled her and then

plunged forward, and in a few strides had disappeared into the trees.

"I'm so glad he's safe," the White Cat said in relief.

"Me too," agreed Holly, pushing the thoughts of her real life back deep into her mind.

"And now it is our turn to go."

Holly turned and saw that the sylphs had arrived and were standing behind them. Ava walked over. "This is where we must say goodbye."

She and the other sylphs danced around Holly and the White Cat in a shifting, shimmering line and then vanished.

"Goodbye!" Holly called. She sighed, her head was spinning. "What an adventure!"

The White Cat grinned at her. "Come on,

let's get back to the palace and tell everyone all about it!"

° ⊙ .* . ☆ ; ⊙ .* . ☆ ; ⊙ .* . ☆ ; ⊙ .* . °

King Tristan and Queen Isabella, the rulers of Enchantia, were delighted to hear that the enchantment on the carousel had been broken and how the sylphs had helped. The King ordered a garden party in celebration.

Everyone rushed around getting everything ready until there were tables in the gardens piled high with food and great pitchers of fruit juice and elderberry cordial. Musicians started playing in the shade of a willow tree and the party started!

People talked and danced on the lawns. Holly and the White Cat spun each other

round and then Holly broke away to dance
with the other people she had met before –
the Lilac Fairy, Little Red Riding Hood,
Bluebeard and Princess Aurelia. It was so
much fun to be surrounded by a laughing
crowd, all celebrating together. Holly
couldn't stop smiling. "I wish the sylphs
had come," she said to the White Cat, as
she rejoined him for a lively polka. "I'm
sure they'd have liked it here."

"I'm not so sure. Some people prefer keeping themselves to themselves," the White Cat told her as they swung around. "That's just the way they are. I wouldn't like to be like that, though. I think you'd miss out on so much!"

Holly was just thinking about that when her feet start to tingle. Her shoes were glowing. "It's time for me to go home!" she cried. "Goodbye, cat! Goodbye, everyone!"

"Goodbye!" she heard them all shout as a myriad colours surrounded her and whisked her away.

Saying Sorry

Holly landed in the street outside the theatre, snowflakes falling on her hair. She shook her head. It was hard to believe that not a second had passed in the real world while she had been away having such an adventure.

Everything came flooding back – the way she had danced on stage before she'd

left, selfishly and not for the rest of the
corps.

The White Cat's words about the sylphs
echoed in her mind: *some people like keeping
themselves to themselves. That's just the way
they are.*

Holly paused. *Is it the
way I am? Do I really
want to be different from
everyone?*

She thought about
how she had felt at the
garden party: dancing,
feeling surrounded by so much laughter,
being part of something – did she really
want to be on the outside, like the sylphs,
just looking in?

No, she thought suddenly. *I don't want to miss out on things.* She turned from the snow. She had some explaining to do.

The first person she saw when she reached the changing rooms was Chloe. There was a central area with sofas and a drinks table. Chloe was pouring out a glass of water and looked upset.

Holly walked straight over. "I'm sorry," she blurted out.

Chloe looked at her in surprise. Holly carried on, her heart beating almost as fast as it had done when she had faced the Wicked Fairy. "You were right. I shouldn't have danced differently. I should have tried to do what everyone else was doing. And I'm really sorry I snapped at you."

Chloe's face broke into a smile. "That's OK. I was just worried that you were going to get told off by Madame Za-Za."

Their eyes met. "Friends?" said Holly anxiously.

"Friends!" said Chloe, hugging her. "I'd better apologise to the others."

Holly's heart sank. She wasn't looking forward to that at all. She went into the other changing room that her class were using, with Chloe at her side. The other girls stopped talking as she walked in.

"I'm sorry," Holly burst out nervously, knowing she should get it over and done with straight away. "I was really stupid to dance like I did. I just got carried away. I promise I won't do it again."

The other girls' faces relaxed.

"That's OK," said Alice. "It's only the dress rehearsal anyway."

"And it *is* easy to get carried away on stage," said Lily. "I almost did three pirouettes instead of two, I was having so much fun!"

"And I was so busy looking at the lights," said Chloe, "that I almost fell over!"

They all laughed and started talking about what it had been like on stage. Holly slipped happily into the group, comparing the best and worst bits. She felt warm and happy; it was almost like being back in Enchantia again.

Her eyes glanced to the door and she caught sight of a tall, elegant figure there. Madame Za-Za! Holly left the others and went over to the dance teacher. "I'm sorry…" she began for the third time.

"I heard," Madame Za-Za broke in softly. "There is no need to say any more, Holly. It is enough for me that you have apologised to your classmates. I know you will not do it again."

"Oh, no, I promise I won't!" Holly said fervently.

"Well done." Madame Za-Za's eyes held hers. "It is not wrong to dance your best,

Holly, or to want to be an individual. I am
sure in the future there will be many times
when you dance solos and can fully show
off your talent, but for now, dance the best
you can as part of a group and enjoy it."

Holly nodded. "I will. I promise."

Madame Za-Za's face creased into a smile
before she clapped her hands. "Five
minutes, girls, and then you need to be
back on stage!"

° ⊚ ∴ ☆ ⊚ ∴ ⋆ ☆ ⊚ ∴ ☆ ⊚ ∴ °

They all lined up. Holly could feel
determination beating through her. She
wanted to make Madame Za-Za and the
others pleased.

"Good luck," Chloe whispered. Holly
grinned at her. "You too!"

The music started, the curtain rose and
suddenly they were dancing on to the
stage. Holly moved in perfect time with the
others. They all swept their arms gracefully
up and down, and began a series of turning
steps that carried them around the stage.
As they spun, dresses swirling, Holly felt
her heart swell with happiness. She was
dancing on stage with her friends and there

was no place she would rather be.

She smiled secretly to herself. *Well, apart from Enchantia, of course!*

Darcey's Magical Masterclass

Bourette

This pretty turn will have you spinning like a carousel!

⊙ ⋆ ☆ ⊙ ⋆ ☆ ⊙ ⋆ ☆ ⊙ ⋆ ⊙

1.
Start with your arms gently bent in front of you and feet in first position. Rise up on to demi-toe.

2.
Raise your arms straight above your head and hold them in an oval shape so your fingertips are almost touching. This is fifth position.

3.
On your demi-toes leading with your right foot, take tiny steps in the smallest circle you can, going round to the right until you are back facing towards the front.

4.
Return your arms to first position and repeat the steps. This time, turn in the opposite direction so you don't get dizzy!

Magic Ballerina™

Holly and the Magic Tiara

It's the christening of Cinderella's baby, Pearl.

But one of the gifts isn't all that it seems…

**Read on for a sneak preview
of Holly's next adventure…**

Holly followed the White Cat to the beautiful lacy cradle tucked in a little alcove. Baby Pearl was wide awake, her blue eyes shining as she looked at the silver rattle she was clutching.

"Her favourite toy!" said the White Cat, throwing a smile at Holly.

A small puppy suddenly hurtled by, wagging its tail and nearly tripping up one of the servants.

"Max, you naughty thing! Get out from under everyone's feet!"

The White Cat chuckled. "Prince Charming bought the puppy for Pearl for when she's older!"

Holly was confused. Usually the shoes brought her to Enchantia if there was a problem to help sort out, yet everything here seemed picture perfect. Although, when she looked carefully, she could see that some of the servants looked a bit worried. She turned to the White Cat, raising her eyebrows. "So what is going on? What do you need me for?"

"Oh Holly, we're all a bit fearful," he began gravely. "You see, Cinderella can't put out of her mind the dreadful events that took place at the christening of her friend, Princess Aurelia."

Holly had met Princess Aurelia – or Sleeping Beauty – before and remembered her story: The Wicked Fairy, who hadn't been invited to Princess Aurelia's christening, had come anyway, crashing in furiously and wrecking everything with a curse about a spinning wheel.

"Of course, every precaution has been taken," the White Cat went on. "I mean, obviously none of the wicked characters of Enchantia have been invited to Pearl's christening, but that is a problem in itself. You see, if the Wicked Fairy finds out that the christening is taking place and she has not been invited *again*, who knows what evil she might wreak…"

°ⓖ ·*· ☆ ⓖ ·*· ☆ ⓖ ·*· ☆ ⓖ ·*· °

Darcey Bussell

Buy more great Magic Ballerina books direct from HarperCollins
at 10% off recommended retail price.
FREE postage and packing in the UK.

Holly and the Dancing Cat	ISBN 978 0 00 732319 7
Holly and the Silver Unicorn	ISBN 978 0 00 732320 3
Holly and the Magic Tiara	ISBN 978 0 00 732321 0
Holly and the Rose Garden	ISBN 978 0 00 732322 7
Holly and the Ice Palace	ISBN 978 0 00 732323 4
Holly and the Land of Sweets	ISBN 978 0 00 732324 1

All priced at £3.99